What Shall We Do With The Body?

Rae Shirley

A SAMUEL FRENCH ACTING EDITION

SAMUEL FRENCH

FOUNDED 1830

SAMUELFRENCH.COM
SAMUELFRENCH-LONDON.CO.UK

FOR PRODUCTION ENQUIRIES

UNITED STATES AND CANADA

Info@SamuelFrench.com

1-866-598-8449

UNITED KINGDOM AND EUROPE

Plays@SamuelFrench-London.co.uk

020-7255-4302

Each title is subject to availability from Samuel French, depending upon country of performance. Please be aware that *WHAT SHALL WE DO WITH THE BODY?* may not be licensed by Samuel French in your territory. Professional and amateur producers should contact the nearest Samuel French office or licensing partner to verify availability.

WHAT SHALL WE DO WITH THE BODY?

A One-Act Comedy

For Two Females and One Male

CHARACTERS

MISS PAULINE TEMPLE . . . . Author of popular
detective novels

MISS WORTHINGTON. . . . . Her secretary

A MAN . . . . Oddly dressed in eye-dazzling
pajamas, a hat and
carrying an umbrella

TIME: The present.

PLACE: A lonely cottage in the country.

WHAT SHALL WE DO WITH THE BODY?

SCENE: A room furnished with the writer's usual para-phernalia; books, table, typewriter, chairs, etc. A cart with drinks and glasses should be downstage for the action of the play. Door upstage center leads to outdoors, and door up left to kitchen.

AT RISE OF CURTAIN: MISS TEMPLE dictates to MISS WORTHINGTON. We hear the occasional mournful howling of the wind outside. MISS TEMPLE, in slacks, is reclining in her easy chair, legs crossed, as she dictates.

MISS TEMPLE. Did you get that last sentence?
MISS WORTHINGTON. *[Mechanically]* Somewhere in the
    house a door slammed.
MISS TEMPLE. Right . . . . now where were we? Ah, yes.
    Detective-Inspector Jelly gazed thoughtfully down at the
    corpse, his gimlet eyes raking the body. Police Constable
    Albert Jones gave his usual obsequious cough before addres-
    sing his superior. *[MISS TEMPLE gives a deep cough and
    changes her voice to a pseudo-baritone]* 'And what d'you
    reckon he died of, sir -- I mean -- to what do you attribute
    the cause of death?'
MISS WORTHINGTON. *[Scribbling furiously]* . . . cause . . .
    of . . . death.
MISS TEMPLE. *[Usual voice]* For answer, Detective Inspector
    Jelly raked the room with his eyes in a vain search for
    clues . . . .
MISS WORTHINGTON. That's twice you've used the word
    'rake,' Miss Temple.
MISS TEMPLE. Twice? Are you sure?
MISS WORTHINGTON. He's raked the body once, and now

he's raking the room.

MISS TEMPLE. M'mmmm . . . yes . . . m'mmm . . . *[She gets up and begins pacing up and down]* Make it 'scanned.' He scanned the body with his eyes -- his hawklike eyes, then touched the body with the tip of his size twelve regulation boot. *[She demonstrates this with a cushion on the floor, then again resumes a deep voice.]* 'This is a tricky one, Constable. If only the body hadn't been decapitated.'

MISS WORTHINGTON. *[Half groaning]* Oh, no! Not again, Miss Temple!

MISS TEMPLE. What d'you mean -- not again?

MISS WORTHINGTON. Only that in your last two books the body was found with its head missing. I mean, your readers might begin to think you were running out of ideas.

MISS TEMPLE. Who is writing this book, Miss Worthington? You -- or me?

MISS WORTHINGTON. *[Subsiding]* Sorry, Miss Temple.

MISS TEMPLE. You do happen to remember -- I hope! -- that my last book 'What Shall We Do With The Body?' won the Crime Writers Award for the best detective novel of the year?

MISS WORTHINGTON. Of course, Miss Temple. How could I forget! *[Offstage, we hear a wild feminine scream of terror. MISS TEMPLE stares, petrified, but MISS WORTH-INGTON is completely oblivious, apparently not hearing anything.]*

MISS TEMPLE. Dear lord!

MISS WORTHINGTON. What's the matter, Miss Temple? Why are you looking like that?

MISS TEMPLE. That scream! Didn't you hear it?

MISS WORTHINGTON. *[Puzzled]* Scream? What scream?

MISS TEMPLE. What scream? You don't mean to say -- you must have heard it!

MISS WORTHINGTON. No. I didn't. I didn't hear a thing.

MISS TEMPLE. *[Incredulously]* You're not deaf, are you?

MISS WORTHINGTON. I assure you, Miss Temple, I am not

deaf.
MISS TEMPLE. Odd . . . crazy. I could have sworn . . . .
MISS WORTHINGTON. *[Delicately]* May I suggest that you are so immersed in your book -- the act of creation -- the -- the -- the --
MISS TEMPLE. *[Impatiently]* -- get on with it, girl. The -- what?
MISS WORTHINGTON. What I'm trying to say, Miss Temple, you have become so lost in your writing -- in your char- acters . . . . if it happens to them, it happens to you. It's all in the mind. In **your** mind, that is. Which is why I didn't hear anything.
MISS TEMPLE. You're not suggesting I'm bonkers, are you?
MISS WORTHINGTON. Certainly not! Bonkers -- really!
MISS TEMPLE. *[Anxious to be convinced]* H'mmm . . . . could be, I suppose, could be.
MISS WORTHINGTON. What other explanation could there be?
MISS TEMPLE. You could be right at that. I do have a strong imagination . . . and I'm psychic, too.
MISS WORTHINGTON. I don't doubt it, Miss Temple.
MISS TEMPLE. *[Briskly]* Well, we won't get the baby bathed this way. Let's get on with it. Ready?
MISS WORTHINGTON. *[Pencil at the ready]* Ready.
MISS TEMPLE. *[In deep voice]* 'Quick,' cried Detective- Inspector Jelly, as he dashed to the door and tried to wrench it open. Police Constable Albert Jones coughed again. *[She coughs, then continues in deep voice]* 'You're pulling it the wrong way, sir,' he said. 'It's marked Push.' 'Then push, you fool!' snarled Jelly. As usual, his ulcer was acting up after the sight of the corpse . . .
MISS WORTHINGTON. Not quite so fast, Miss Temple . . . . 'his ulcer was acting up -- after sight -- of the corpse. . . .
MISS TEMPLE. *[Sighing pointedly, and spacing words]* Police Constable Albert Jones -- pushed open the door -- and there -- before him stood -- the headless body -- of a --

naked woman.

MISS WORTHINGTON. *[Repeating mechanically]* . . . stood the headless body . . . . of a naked woman. *[Almost to herself]* Here we go again.

MISS TEMPLE. *[Sharply]* Did you say something, Miss Worthington?

MISS WORTHINGTON. *[Blandly]* I only repeated what you just dictated, Miss Temple. *[MISS TEMPLE paces up and down. MISS WORTHINGTON returns to her notes.]* You did say 'stood?' 'The headless body stood?'

MISS TEMPLE. *[Burps slightly, pats her chest]* Pardon me. What did you say?

MISS WORTHINGTON. This headless body, you left it standing up. Is that right?

MISS TEMPLE. Of course it's right. Why shouldn't it stand on its own two feet?

MISS WORTHINGTON. If you say so, Miss Temple . . . but . .

MISS TEMPLE. -- but -- what? What is it now, Miss Worthington?

MISS WORTHINGTON. I only wondered -- as a matter of curiosity -- how can a headless body keep standing up?

MISS TEMPLE. *[Triumphantly]* A-a-aah! There lies the craft of the crime writer, Miss Worthington. **You're** wondering! My readers will be wondering! **Everybody** will be wondering!

MISS WORTHINGTON. The critics might be wondering -- especially the medical ones.

MISS TEMPLE. *[Scornfully]* Them! Who cares! *[More thoughtfully]* H'mmm . . . come to think of it, it does present a bit of a problem . . . yes . . . I'll work it out, of course.

MISS WORTHINGTON. Of course.

MISS TEMPLE. H'mmm . . . basically, it's a question of balance. How can a headless body resist the law of gravity so that it remains in the upright position?

MISS WORTHINGTON. To Stand -- Or Not to Stand? That

is the question.

MISS TEMPLE. *[Suspiciously]* You putting me on or something?

MISS WORTHINGTON. Oh, no, Miss Temple. Certainly not!

MISS TEMPLE. Because I tell you, here and now, Miss Worthington, don't try. My brother tried it once too often -- just the once, but **never** again. He couldn't. Physical impossibility -- however, we won't go into that. Now, where were we? Oh, yes. Upright bodies. The medical dictionary. Get it.

MISS WORTHINGTON. *[Flies to the bookcase, takes out a large volume]* Here you are, Miss Temple.

MISS TEMPLE. Don't give it to me, woman. Look it up!

MISS WORTHINGTON. Look it up? Look what up?

MISS TEMPLE. Really, Miss Worthington! We are not with it this evening, are we? Headless bodies, of course.

MISS WORTHINGTON. *[Eyes heavenwards]* Of course! *[As she rapidly turns over the pages]* Headless bodies . . . headless bodies . . . . heatstroke . . . heart attack . . . heartburn . . hernia . . . *[Looking up from the book]* Nothing here about headless bodies, Miss Temple.

MISS TEMPLE. That dictionary's a bit out-of-date, of course. I'll have to get a new one. Oh, well, never mind. My doctor will probably have some ideas. He's always been most helpful in the past.

MISS WORTHINGTON. *[Inspired]* I know!

MISS TEMPLE. Well?

MISS WORTHINGTON. What about having the murderer standing behind the naked headless woman? Sort of propping her up?

MISS TEMPLE. *[Closing her eyes as if trying to visualize it]* No . . . no . . . I can't see the picture . . . .

MISS WORTHINGTON. *[Jumps up and tries to demonstrate]* If you'll kindly stand up . . . . thank you. *[She stands behind MISS TEMPLE, apparently supporting her from behind.]* Something like this. Now, I'm the murderer . . .

and you're the headless naked woman. Do you see what
I'm getting at?
MISS TEMPLE. M'mmmm . . . doubtful . . . . very doubtful.
He'd have to be a very short murderer, wouldn't he? I mean,
the corpse is a woman -- naked -- so she wouldn't be that
tall -- not without her head.
MISS WORTHINGTON. You could give her high-heeled shoes.
That would make her taller. And if he were a short little
murderer . . .
MISS TEMPLE. *[Thoughtfully]* A short little murderer. A
dwarf, perhaps . . . ?
MISS WORTHINGTON. A dwarf! That's positively brilliant,
Miss Temple!
MISS TEMPLE. *[With assumed modesty]* I admit, it is quite
a good idea. It would give it a touch of the . . . the . . .
MISS WORTHINGTON. -- macabre?
MISS TEMPLE. That's it -- that's the word. Macabre. Yes, I
can see it now. It's dramatic! Exciting! Visual!
MISS WORTHINGTON. It's visual, all right.
MISS TEMPLE. And I don't believe it's been done before.
Not all three together, I mean. A dwarf, a headless corpse,
and a naked woman. *[Offstage we hear another wild fem-
inine scream of terror]* Suffering Judas! There it is again!
MISS WORTHINGTON. There is what again?
MISS TEMPLE. I must be dreaming this! You didn't hear it?
MISS WORTHINGTON. Oh, no, Miss Temple! Not another
silent scream?
MISS TEMPLE. Silent? Hah! I must have gremlins inside my
skull, and they're all screaming. *[Uncertainly]* I know I
heard something.
MISS WORTHINGTON. *[Lightly]* Well, it can't be your
headless woman, can it? You can't scream without a head!
MISS TEMPLE. *[Shuddering]* Don't! You're giving me the
purple shudders. *[She paces back and forth.]*
MISS WORTHINGTON. *[Jumping and giving faint scream]*
Oh -- now I heard it. O-ooh, ... it sounds like a soul in·

torment.

MISS TEMPLE. Now she's got gremlins in her skull! I know I shouldn't have taken this lonely cottage out in the country. The place is haunted. You heard something . . . no, don't tell me. It was a woman screaming. Right?

MISS WORTHINGTON. Yes, yes, of course I heard it. Did you hear it?

MISS TEMPLE. Not then, I didn't. This is going to bring on my heart condition. Gallops away like mad . . . can't keep up with it. *[Another wild scream. MISS TEMPLE DROPS her manuscript]* Oh, My God!

MISS WORTHINGTON. You've dropped your papers.

MISS TEMPLE. Did you hear it then?

MISS WORTHINGTON. Hear what?

MISS TEMPLE. The scream, idiot, the scream?

MISS WORTHINGTON. *[Nonplussed]* No. I've only heard it once -- and once was more than enough.

MISS TEMPLE. Only once? I've heard it -- is it three times -- or four! *[She turns to pour herself a drink with a trembling hand. While she is doing this, there is a loud knock on the door. The two WOMEN gaze at each other, both fearful.]*

MISS WORTHINGTON. I heard that!

MISS TEMPLE. So did I.

MISS WORTHINGTON. Who -- who could it be this time of night? May I -- may I have a little . . . *[She indicates drinks. MISS TEMPLE pours one for her, and hands her the drink. Another shattering knock. Both drink.]*

MISS TEMPLE. Perhaps -- perhaps it's that poor woman?

MISS WORTHINGTON. What poor woman?

MISS TEMPLE. The one who was screaming.

MISS WORTHINGTON. I'd forgotten about her.

MISS TEMPLE. I hadn't. Well . . . I'm waiting, Miss Worthington.

MISS WORTHINGTON. Waiting, Miss Temple?

MISS TEMPLE. For you to answer the door.

MISS WORTHINGTON. *[Approaches the door fearfully. She*

hesitates. There is another knock. She turns towards MISS TEMPLE.] I -- I don't feel very well.

[MISS TEMPLE takes a hasty swallow of her drink, picks up a ruler from near the typewriter, sweeps MISS WORTHINGTON aside, and flings open the door. MISS WORTHINGTON is now standing behind the door, so does not see the MAN standing there. He is dressed in eye-dazzling pajamas, on his arm a rolled umbrella. His hat has momentarily slipped over his face, and for a fleeting moment, he appears to be headless. MISS TEMPLE gives a despairing groan, and promptly sinks to the floor in a dead faint. MISS WORTHINGTON leaps out, kneels down, and supports MISS TEMPLE's head, fanning her with a kleenex.]

MISS WORTHINGTON. Oh, Miss Temple, Miss Temple! *[She looks up at the MAN who has by now stepped tentatively inside the doorway. His hat is smacked squarely on top of his head.]* You brute! What have you done to her?
MAN. I didn't do anything -- I swear! She took one look at me, and -- oh, dear! I've never had this effect on women before!
MISS WORTHINGTON. Stop chattering and give me something to fan her with. *[He hands her his hat and she fans vigorously]* **Do** something, can't you? Get a drink or something.
MAN. Thanks. I will. *[He goes quickly to the cart, pours out a drink and swallows it. A loud groan from MISS TEMPLE]*
MISS WORTHINGTON. She's coming round. Help me get her into a chair. *[Together, they lift her awkwardly and stumble with her to a chair. Gaspingly:]* Oh, dear! She really will have to try and stick to her diet.
MISS TEMPLE. O-oooh! Where am I? Wha -- what's happened?
MISS WORTHINGTON. You fainted, Miss Temple.
MISS TEMPLE. *[Sitting up in chair]* Fainted? I never faint!

I've never fainted in my life. *[As she suddenly catches sight of the man, she screams]* Wha -- what's that?

MISS WORTHINGTON. *[Soothingly]* It's only a man, my dear.

MAN. I don't know why I keep having this effect on her. Doesn't she like men?

MISS WORTHINGTON. *[Acidly]* Who does!

MISS TEMPLE. *[Pointing at him]* I remember! He's got a head now. When I saw him standing in the doorway, he didn't have a head.

MISS WORTHINGTON. Really . . . you've been working too hard.

MISS TEMPLE. Well, there could have been someone standing behind him -- like you said.

MISS WORTHINGTON. I assure you, he's got a head. *[To MAN]* Here a minute. *[He goes to her, and she taps him briskly on the head.]* There! That's solid enough.

MAN. *[Trying to be helpful]* Perhaps it was my hat. It's too large for me, and it dropped over my face when the door opened.

MISS TEMPLE. You see, Miss Worthington? I am not imagining things. Working too hard, indeed! You'll be saying I'm a mental case next!

MISS WORTHINGTON. I'm sorry. I didn't mean --

MISS TEMPLE. *[Interrupting]* -- what's he doing here, anyway? And in his pajamas, too.

MISS WORTHINGTON. *[Mildly surprised]* In his pajamas? So he is!

MISS TEMPLE. Really! It's about time you changed your glasses!

MISS WORTHINGTON. I thought it was a very light suit for this time of the year.

MAN. I do apologize for my unconventional attire. I had to leave in a hurry.

MISS TEMPLE. Leave?

MAN. My cottage. It burned down. All I could salvage was

my hat and my umbrella. One must keep up his appearance.

MISS TEMPLE. Cottage, cottage? But there isn't another cottage within a radius of ten miles.

MAN. Fifteen. I walked.

MISS TEMPLE. You walked? Did you hear that, Miss Worthington? He walked for fifteen miles! Er -- you -- er -- didn't happen to see a woman on your way here?

MAN. A woman? Out alone? At this time of night? I certainly didn't.

MISS TEMPLE. Or -- perhaps -- even hear a woman . . . ?

MAN. Hear her?

MISS TEMPLE. Screaming.

MAN. Good heavens, no! Certainly not.

MISS WORTHINGTON. There you are, Miss Temple. No cause for alarm.

MAN. Pardon me, but did I hear the name -- Temple?

MISS TEMPLE. That's my name.

MAN. Not **the** Pauline Temple? The famous detective writer?

MISS TEMPLE. *[Preening]* The same!

MAN. But this is marvelous! That wonderful book -- 'The Corpse Without a Coffin' . . . the suspense, the skill, the -- words fail me! What an honor to be actually talking to so illustrious an author!

MISS TEMPLE. Well . . . thank you, Mr. -- er -- rum – er -- rum . . . .

MAN. Tell me, Miss Temple, how do you get your ideas? Oh, what a gift! You know, I've always wanted to write, but alas! It's all up here - *[He taps his head]* - burning to be written . . . but trying to transfer it onto that blank white page . . . *[He shakes his head]* I know how difficult it is. I can appreciate and admire someone like you who has -- such proficiency in the art of story telling.

MISS WORTHINGTON. He's spreading it on thick, isn't he?

MISS TEMPLE. Flattery, indeed, Mr. -- er -- rum -- er - rum --

MAN. No, no, no! Not flattery, my dear Miss Temple. I

speak from the heart, and the heart cannot lie. Oh, dear . . .
[He sways] . . I feel a little . . .
MISS TEMPLE. Oh, how very thoughtless of me . . . the poor
man must be dropping for a warm drink and something to
eat. Do go and make a cup of your nice coffee, Miss Worth-
ington, and perhaps a sandwich or two.
MISS WORTHINGTON. *[Flatly]* We haven't any bread.
MISS TEMPLE. Oh, well, then biscuits, cheese, anything.

*[MISS WORTHINGTON exits, sullenly. MISS TEMPLE
continues, apologetically]*

You must excuse her. She means well, but I'm afraid . . .
[She taps her head significantly] . . . I happen to know we
have plenty of bread. Brown and white.
MAN. *[With sudden change of manner, conspiratorially]*
Miss Temple, may I take you into my confidence?
MISS TEMPLE. Into your confidence? What do you mean,
Mr. -- er -- rum -- er -- rum . . . .
MAN. I need help in the execution of my duties, but . . . *[He
glances around the room apprehensively]* . . . First I must
have your word that I can trust you.
MISS TEMPLE. But, Mr. -- er -- rum -- er -- rum . . . .
MAN. The fact is -- I am not what you think I am.
MISS TEMPLE. You mean -- you're not a **Man!?**
MAN. Yes, yes, of course I'm a man, but -- the fact is -- these
pajamas are a blind.
MISS TEMPLE. Well, the colors are sort of ----
MAN. *[Lowering voice furtively]* Special Branch, like the
CIA. S'SHhhhhhhh!
MISS TEMPLE. *[Stage whispering too]* Special Branch.
S'Sssshhhh! *[Light dawning and raising her voice]* Oh,
Special Branch! I know all about them. My books, you
know.
MAN. S'sssshhhhh!
MISS TEMPLE. Double O Seven?

MAN. Double Seven O.

MISS TEMPLE. *[Thrilled]* Really? Double Seven O!

MAN. S'sshhhh! Seal your lips, Miss Temple. Secrecy must be our watchword.

MISS TEMPLE. Secrecy -- Watchword. By all means, Mr. -- er --

MAN. S'ssh . . . no names!

MISS TEMPLE. No names -- of course. I'll remember. But, why the secrecy?

MAN. *[Impatiently]* My mission, of course.

MISS TEMPLE. Mission . . . oh. Er -- what precisely is your mission, Double Seven O?

MAN. *[Jerking thumb in direction of MISS WORTHINGTON's exit]* Can you trust -- her?

MISS TEMPLE. Her? Oh, you mean Miss Worthington? Well, frankly, she's naive, if you get what I mean, but I can trust her. She's too simple to be anything but honest.

MAN. *[Darkly insinuating]* I wonder . . . how long has she been with you?

MISS TEMPLE. Oh, a considerable time.

MAN. How long is that?

MISS TEMPLE. Let me see . . . now, where is my diary? I have a shocking memory, you know. I only remember my books. Today . . . ? Oh, yes . . . today is Thursday, isn't it? . . . yes . . . she arrived the day before yesterday.

MAN. The day before yester -- and you call that a considerable time?

MISS TEMPLE. Everything is relative, Mr. er -- rum -- I mean, Seven Double O. None of my secretaries ever stay more than three days. They say I work them too hard. Lazy creatures! This one hasn't complained. Not yet, anyway.

MAN. *[Cunningly]* Did she have good references?

MISS TEMPLE. I wouldn't know. I never ask for them. I can sum up a person's character at a glance. Well, say, two glances.

MAN. Well, you may be right, but . . . .

MISS TEMPLE. But . . . . . ?
MAN. Did you know that a patient has escaped from the
    Broadley Nursing Home?
MISS TEMPLE. The insane asylum?
MAN. Right!
MISS TEMPLE. *[Quickly]* When?
MAN. I hate to say this . . .
MISS TEMPLE. Go on, go on!
MAN. The day before yesterday.
MISS TEMPLE. You don't mean – you can't mean -- that --
MAN. I am afraid so, Miss Temple.
MISS TEMPLE. Not -- not -- Miss Worthington?
MAN. Herself.
MISS TEMPLE. I can't believe it.
MAN. But, surely, you must have noticed something about
    her, something out of the ordinary?
MISS TEMPLE. *[Dazed]* Out of the ordinary?
MAN. Sort of odd. Unbalanced.
MISS TEMPLE. Unbalanced? Yes, come to think of it . . . it
    didn't quite register at the time, but . . .
MAN. But . . . ?
MISS TEMPLE. When you said unbalanced, it struck a bell.
    Her idea of balance for a headless body -- my book, you
    know. Extremely odd.
MAN. I'm not surprised.
MISS TEMPLE. And when I suggested -- as a kind of joke,
    really -- to look up headless body in the medical diction-
    ary -- she actually did. The more I think of it . . . .
MAN. Typical of her case, typical. When I tell Dr. Gregory . . .
    [Shakes his head] Most disturbing, but typical.
MISS TEMPLE. *[Nervously]* I don't mind this sort of situation
    in my books, but in real life . . . it's so different, isn't it?
MAN. It's different, all right. Not to put too fine a point on
    it, Miss Temple, your Miss Worthington has homicidal tend-
    encies.
MISS TEMPLE. Homicidal --- oh no! And she seems to have

a weakness for headless bodies!

MAN. *[Grimly]* Correct. She has.

MISS TEMPLE. How -- how do you know?

MAN. That's her method.

MISS TEMPLE. *[Faintly]* Method?

MAN. Thirteen.

MISS TEMPLE. Thirteen?

MAN. Her method of getting rid of them. She's stuck at thirteen.

MISS TEMPLE. *[Fearfully]* Stuck?

MAN. That's right. And she's terribly superstitious, so she's bound to have another.

MISS TEMPLE. Another . . . . ?

MAN. Another body.

MISS TEMPLE. Oh, dear! I feel rather . . .

MAN. Headless, of course.

MISS TEMPLE. Of course!

MAN. And you really hadn't suspected anything?

MISS TEMPLE. Nothing like **that**! If I had . . . .

MAN. I only wondered. You did say you could sum up a person's character at a glance.

MISS TEMPLE. Well, that's the ordinary person, the man or woman in the street. I am not in the habit of meeting homicidal maniacs. What are we going to do?

MAN. *[Walking up and down with slow deliberate steps, using his umbrella as a walking-stick]* Strategy. We need strategy. She's cunning. Dead cunning, if you'll pardon the expression. They all are.

MISS TEMPLE. Schizophrenia.

MAN. I beg your pardon?

MISS TEMPLE. Schizophrenia. Split personality and all that.

MAN. Oh, that! Oh, yes, definitely. Without a doubt.

MISS TEMPLE. Must you keep walking up and down all the time? You're making me dizzy.

MAN. I'm trying to think. I always think better in motion.

MISS TEMPLE. Well, put your umbrella down.

MAN. I'd rather not, if you don't mind. It helps me - *[He touches his head]* - up here.

MISS TEMPLE. I know what helps me. *[She goes to help herself to a drink]* Would you care for one?

MAN. I never drink on duty. Against the rules.

MISS TEMPLE. I always drink on duty. Writer's rules.

MAN. *[Explosively, and suddenly arrested in his stride]* Do you have a gun?

MISS TEMPLE. A gun? Let me think. Yes, yes . . . I've got one somewhere. *[She puts her drink down and goes to sideboard or bureau and begins to rummage about.]* At least, I thought I had . . . *[In sudden alarm]* -- you don't think -- she can't have taken it, has she?

MAN. Heaven help us if she has!

MISS TEMPLE. Heaven help us, indeed. I always keep it loaded.

MAN. Let me look.

MISS TEMPLE. Ah, here it is. What a relief!

MAN. Relief is right. This will cut short her career!

MISS TEMPLE. I sincerely hope so.

MAN. Now, if you will kindly let me have it -- the gun.

MISS TEMPLE. Gladly. *[She is about to hand it over, then pauses]* I wonder . . . .

MAN. This is no time to wonder. Give me the gun.

MISS TEMPLE. But, we haven't decided on a plan of campaign. What are we going to **do**?

MAN. Confront her, of course. Tell her the game is up.

MISS TEMPLE. If I cover her with the gun, you can still do that.

MAN. With the gun in my hand, I could be a little more -- persuasive, shall we say? So, be a good girl and give me that gun.

[MISS WORTHINGTON enters, carrying a tray with coffee pot, milk, cups or mugs, etc.]

MISS WORTHINGTON. Sorry to have been so long. The
  stove got temperamental.
MAN. *[Sotto voce]*   The gun, the gun!
MISS WORTHINGTON. I had to use thirteen matches . . . 13!
  Most unfortunate!
MISS TEMPLE. *[With frightened glance at man]* Unfortunate?
MISS WORTHINGTON. The number thirteen. It has sinister
  undertones. Surely you know that. I hate to be stuck at
  thirteen. *[She attends to pouring out coffee. Then, to
  MAN]* I'm used to electric stoves, of course. Gas makes
  me nervous. Explosions and things. Black or white?
MAN. Black.
MISS TEMPLE. None for me, thank you. I'm relying on
  something stronger.
MISS WORTHINGTON. *[Takes a cup of coffee to the MAN.
  He starts to sip it.]* I've been listening to a police message
  on the radio. Do you know a patient has escaped from the
  Broadley Asylum?   *[MISS TEMPLE takes a hasty gulp of
  her drink. The MAN chokes over his coffee. MISS WORTH-
  INGTON sits down with her coffee. Then, airily:]* Not
  that that sort of thing worries me much.
MISS TEMPLE. It doesn't?
MISS WORTHINGTON. No. I've spent far too much time in
  asylums to worry over a little thing like that.
MISS TEMPLE. Too much time? You mean -- you were a
  patient?
MISS WORTHINGTON. No way! Whatever gave you that
  idea? That's funny! Wait till Dr. Peabody hears that one!
MISS TEMPLE. Dr. Peabody?
MAN. He is the -- ah -- resident medical superintendent at
  Broadley, I believe.
MISS WORTHINGTON. *[Meaningly]* You mean he **was**!
  But -- something happened to him. The coroner's verdict
  was accidental death, but some of us knew better.
MISS TEMPLE. But -- but if he's not there any longer -- Dr.
  Peabody -- how can you tell him what you said you were

going to tell him?

MISS WORTHINGTON. Ways and means, Miss Temple, ways and means. I'll never forget the time I was a male nurse.

MAN. *[Edging close to MISS TEMPLE, out of the corner of his mouth]* The gun, the gun!

MISS WORTHINGTON. When we had the costume party, New Year's Eve. Very original. The patients didn't like it, though. It seemed to confuse them. I can't think why.

MAN. I -- I wonder -- might I trouble you for a little more sugar?

MISS WORTHINGTON. Sugar? But, I've already put two teaspoonsful in.

MAN. I take three.

MISS WORTHINGTON. Really? You've got a sweet tooth, haven't you?

MAN. A mouthful of them.

MISS WORTHINGTON. Sugar bowl's empty. I'll have to get some more.

[She exits.]

MISS TEMPLE. She's regressing fast.

MAN. Regressing? She's gone! Quick, keep a lookout. I'm going to put something in her coffee.

MISS TEMPLE. *[Delighted]* Poison?

MAN. Don't be ridiculous! We want to capture her, not bury her. *[He fumbles in his pocket, and drops tablets onto floor. They both scramble about on all fours looking for them.]* Where the -- can you see them?

MISS TEMPLE. I think they rolled under the chair . . . oh, here we are.

MAN. Quick! *[They scramble up, he pulling her up with him]* Into her cup.

MISS TEMPLE. It's a large capsule, isn't it?

MAN. It needs to be! It has a very large purpose.

MISS TEMPLE. *[With anxious glance towards door]* What

will it do to her?

MAN. Knock her out, I hope -- but she's a tough nut. Now, give me that gun.

MISS TEMPLE. All right, all right!

[She starts to hand him the gun, drops it, and it is thrown into the center of the stage . . . just as MISS WORTHING-TON enters with the sugar bowl.]

MISS WORTHINGTON. Oh! A gun! *[She picks it up and goes toward the MAN with the sugar bowl. He helps him-self to sugar nervously, his eyes rivetted on the gun.]* What are we playing? Cowboys and Indians? *[Pause]* Why are you both staring at me like that? *[She goes back to her cup of coffee and places the gun carelessly beside her. They both watch fascinated.]* Is anything the matter? The silence is deafening. *[She picks up her cup, is about to drink some coffee, but puts it down again.]* I was just thinking . . . . that headless woman . . .

MISS TEMPLE. W-w-what headless woman?

MISS WORTHINGTON. The one we left standing outside the door with a dwarf propping her up.

MISS TEMPLE. *[Nervous laugh]* Oh -- **that** one!

MISS WORTHINGTON. Couldn't we make it a headless man?

MAN. *[Sotto voce]* Humor her, for God's sake!

MISS WORTHINGTON. *[To MAN]* Did you say something?

MAN. *[Hastily]* No, no! A frog in my throat.

MISS TEMPLE. I -- I'll think about it.

MISS WORTHINGTON. Oh, well, suit yourself. It was just an idea. You're the murderer -- I mean, writer. O-ooh, this coffee is terribly hot. I almost burnt my tongue.

MAN. That's the way I like my coffee. Very hot and burning the tongue.

MISS WORTHINGTON. I don't. Gives me heartburn.

MAN. *[His hand hovering over gun]* Let me help you to a little milk.

MISS WORTHINGTON. *[Knocking his hand away]* No, no, no! I like mine black. *[She looks intently at him.]* You know, there is something strangely familiar about you.
MAN. *[Nervously]* About me? Surely not!
MISS WORTHINGTON. Yes. Definitely. It's your face . . . I think . . . yes . . . that nose. I've never seen a nose quite like it -- except on you, of course. *[She gets up and walks toward him as he retreats.]* Yes. No doubt about it. It's your nose.
MAN. *[Touching nose nervously]* It's just an ordinary nose. Thousands like it.
MISS WORTHINGTON. A-a-aah! But that's where you're wrong. If there were thousands like it, why should it stand out like it does?
MAN. Well, a nose is supposed to stand out, isn't it? I mean to say, all noses do.
MISS WORTHINGTON. Yours is different, I tell you. I'm sure we've met somewhere before.
MAN. No, no. Positively not.
MISS WORTHINGTON. I could have sworn . . . it wasn't Peoria?
MAN. No.
MISS WORTHINGTON. Could it have been Nome?
MAN. No -- never -- no!
MISS WORTHINGTON. Topeka! Of course, that's where it was. Don't you remember? At that -- well, they called it a clinic, but --
MAN. *[Interrupting desperately]* -- Madam, I assure you, I have never seen you before in my life!
MISS WORTHINGTON. Ah, well, they say we all have doubles, don't they? *[She looks at him intently for a moment, then returns to her coffee.]* Strange, very strange.
MISS TEMPLE. After all that, I think you both deserve a little pick-up. *[She goes to the cart, her own drink still in her hand. She pours two drinks, her back to the others, but facing audience. She drops something into both glasses.]*

MAN. You haven't had your coffee yet, Miss Worthington.

MISS WORTHINGTON. No sooner said than done. *[She drains the cup.]* I do make a good cup of coffee. At least . . . *[She looks doubtfully at her cup]* . . I thought I did. That tasted a little funny.

MISS TEMPLE. *[Takes the drink over to the MAN, giving him a conspiratorial look, taking drink also to MISS WORTHINGTON. She picks up the gun lying on the table.]* I don't like to see firearms lying around, do you? Especially when they're loaded. Makes me nervous. I mean, you never know, do you? You'll have to excuse me a moment. Most urgent!

[She throws the MAN a meaningful glance and makes a quick exit. The MAN makes to follow her, but MISS WORTHINGTON lifts a warning hand.]

MISS WORTHINGTON. *[In stage whisper]* Let her go, you fool!

MAN. Are you mad? She's got the gun!

MISS WORTHINGTON. *[Succinctly]* Blanks!

MAN. *[Mopping fevered brow]* I wish to God I'd known that before. Why didn't you give me the tip-off when she fainted?

MISS WORTHINGTON. Fainted -- her? Don't make me laugh! That's one of her favorite tricks!

MAN. I might have known! Has she got any live bullets?

MISS WORTHINGTON. Not now, she hasn't. I flushed them down.

MAN. Talking of guns, there's something I wanted to ask you . . . oh, my poor throat! You got any lozenges?

MISS WORTHINGTON. What's the matter with your throat?

MAN. All that screaming I had to do -- and soprano, too. My vocal chords are in shreds.

MISS WORTHINGTON. Here, suck this. *[She hands him a cough drop.]* What did you want to ask me?

MAN. Rot -- can't remember . . . .
MISS WORTHINGTON. Is it important?
MAN. Of course it's important. My brain's completely addled.
MISS WORTHINGTON. Stop worrying. It'll come back.
MAN. *[Looking under carpet, behind pictures, etc.]* You're
    sure the place isn't bugged?
MISS WORTHINGTON. *[Trying to be patient]* It is not bug-
    ged -- not now. Is that what you wanted to ask me?
MAN. It might have been. I'm not sure. I had a couple of
    bad moments when I thought she was catching on.
MISS WORTHINGTON. Can't always tell, not with her kind.
    D'you reckon she believed you when you said you were
    from the Special Branch?
MAN. Oh, yes. That one really got to her. The result of all
    those make-believe books she writes.
MISS WORTHINGTON. What's the idea of the pajamas?
    When I saw you, it all but threw me.
MAN. You can thank the Boss for that.
MISS WORTHINGTON. Dr. Peabody? I don't believe it.
MAN. I tell you, it was. He said the sight of a man in his
    pajamas always raised the motherly instinct in a woman.
MISS WORTHINGTON. You could've fooled me! *[She picks
    up her coffee cup]* Good Lord! What on earth did you put
    in my coffee?
MAN. All I had on me. Life Savers!
MISS WORTHINGTON. Life Savers! Honestly, George!
    You're some detective!
MAN. You should talk! Giving me all that Peoria, Nome,
    Topeka routine. We never rehearsed that. It could have
    switched suspicion onto me.
MISS WORTHINGTON. Well, obviously it didn't. If anything,
    it put her off guard. She doesn't know where she is now.
MAN. Frankly, I'm beginning to wonder myself.
MISS WORTHINGTON. I don't know what you're grumbling
    about. I've had to live with her these past two days -- and
    there's no lock on my bedroom door.

MAN. I wish I could remember what it was I wanted to check
  with you. *[He beats his head]* It was the last thing the
  Boss said to me. It's vital you check with Miss Worthing-
  ton, I remember him saying.
MISS WORTHINGTON. If it's that vital, you ought to remem-
  ber it.
MAN. I **know** I ought to, but I don't.
MISS WORTHINGTON. Is it about the van? That's safe, I
  hope.
MAN. Of course it's safe. How do you think I got here?
  Walked?
MISS WORTHINGTON. The straitjacket? Did you remember
  to bring that?
MAN. The questions you do ask! It's all ready in the driver's
  seat.
MISS WORTHINGTON. That's okay, then. Cheer up, it's
  nearly over now. I'm going to have this drink she so
  obligingly poured for us.
MAN. You're right. I worry too much. Always did. I'll have
  to have another spell down on that health farm.
MISS WORTHINGTON. I'll come with you, if the Boss can
  spare me. I could do with some relaxation after this. Let's
  drink to tonight's work and success. The Boss will be
  pleased it's ended so well.
MAN. He's not the only one. I feel like a fool in these pajamas.
  Cheers!
MISS WORTHINGTON. Cheers! *[They both drink up.]*
MAN. I'll say this for her -- she knows a good whiskey . . . she
  knows a good . . . *[His eyes become staring and glassy]*
  My God! It's come back to me! I've remembered!
MISS WORTHINGTON. *[Looking likewise]* What is it?
  What is it?
MAN. The hatchet! Did you remember to bury the hatchet?
MISS WORTHINGTON. The hatchet! Oh, my God! The
  hatchet!

[They both sink to the floor unconscious. MISS TEMPLE enters, carrying a hatchet, with a brisk and businesslike air. She looks down at them, almost regretfully, shaking her head.]

MISS TEMPLE. Such a waste -- two of them! I only wanted one to make it fourteen. *[She raises the hatchet . . . .]*

[CURTAIN – THE END]